Fan Mail

Femdom Hypnosis and Mind Control Micro-Fiction

S.B.

The truth is in the mail.

A special thank to all patrons of Spell... B-O-U-N-D.

Table of Contents

Introduction

Women know better than you. They always have, they always will. Sometimes, you fail to acknowledge it, but that is okay. They have ways to remind you and take control of your thoughts whenever they want.

You are a fan of dominant women, their toy, their pet. It is all you can be. The truth is you are born to obey, and you will. This collection of entrancing micro-fiction will show you just how much power they really have. Have fun.

Behavioral Correction

"You're late!" Hannah exclaimed. "That's the third time this week! If you don't get your act together, I'll have no choice but to find myself a new servant!"

"Please, no… anything but that! I beg you!" Jonathan kneeled at her feet.

"Oh, you'll most certainly beg..." She grinned. "But first… look deep into my eyes…"

The Awakening

The chambers glowed eerily, inciting the explorers to enter them and let go… Inside, thoughts slowly melted away, replaced by deviant conceptions of reality. A new purpose was given to them as well as the necessary knowledge to see it through. Upon release, they traveled deeper inside the spaceship, to awaken their Mistresses from stasis.

Finner is Servef

"What's for dinner, Joe?" Ginger asked.

"Fuck a l'Orange," he blurted.

"Skipping foreplay, are you?"

"Fedinitely not! Huh, why am I talking like this?"

"Because you're a very good hypnotic subject. Now tell me you want to fuck me."

"I want to duck you," he said, embarrassed.

"Don't forget the orange juice, dear," she smirked.

All of It

Kafka's words echoed inside Jonah's mind as he stared into Rachel's eyes.

"You are at once both the quiet and the confusion of my heart," he repeated them out loud.

"What do you prefer most?" She inquired as she continued to weave her spell.

"All of it," he exhaled sleepy surrender before drifting into silence.

Slave Blogger

Daniel sighed. Blogging was hard when he felt he had nothing to say, and the keyboard mocked him at every turn.

Taking a deep breath, he glanced at the blinking icon on the taskbar. Therein, the gateway to his only source of inspiration.

"Obey," Janice's voice penetrated his mind.

He acquiesced and began to write.

A Long Time Ago, In a Galaxy Far, Far Away...

Star Wars Episode LXIX - Rinse and Repeat

We continue to try to milk the franchise. There's a new Empire, a new Resistance, danger everywhere... the usual stuff. At least the bad guy is a bad girl now and uses the Dark Side of the Force to condition everyone into believing this is worth watching. Enjoy!

No Cock

"No way! There's no fucking way!" Clark screamed.

"Dude!" Jackson intervened. "You'll wake up everyone in the dorm. What's wrong?"

"My cock is gone, that's what's wrong! I can't find it anywhere!"

"Your cock is right the... wait, Amelia hypnotized you again at the party last night, didn't she?"

"Maybe..." she grinned across the hall.

Not Brainwashed

“Come on, Harriet! I’m not brainwashed!” Dave exclaimed.

“Really? Then complete these sentences: Chloe is my…”

“… mistress.”

“I am her…”

“… slave.”

“I must…”

“… obey her.”

“I do not…”

“… argue.”

“Still think you’re not brainwashed, Dave?”

“I… well… maybe I’m a little…”

“… slut for Chloe.”

“What?”

“I’m a little slut for Chloe,” Harriet droned.

Dave laughed.

Resident Sexy 4 Remistressed

Leon stopped to catch his breath.

"What're ya buyin, stranger?" the merchant asked.

"Do you have any Ashley Repellent on you?" Leon begged.

"He doesn't, but I have some mind-warping pheromones..." a sultry voice said.

"Ada?"

"Call me 'Mistress', handsome."

"Selling ya mind, I see," the merchant nodded, feeling dizzy. He could do that, too.

Don't Remember

"Come on, Jade, you promised!"

"Did I?"

"Yes! You said you would let me cum if I cleaned the house today!"

"Don't remember that, Luke."

"You said the same thing yesterday!"

"Don't remember that either."

"Don't remember? Have you been using self-hypnosis again?"

"Huh? What's that?"

"Fuck!"

She laughed. He was so gullible when under.

Only Dreams

"How long have you been having these dreams?" Dr. Hanson asked.

"Three weeks," Josh mumbled.

"Tell me more."

"I… come to your office, you hypnotize me and then fuck my ass on this desk," he blushed.

"Hot but they're only dreams, right?"

"Yes."

"Good," she waved a strap-on before his eyes. His mind went blank.

Another Pet

"You were right, Tamsin," Veronica said.

"About…?"

"I needed a pet in my life."

"Did you get a dog or something?"

"See for yourself."

Tamsin's husband came crawling, wagging his imaginary tail.

"What did you do?" She shrieked.

"Hypnotized him. You don't approve?"

"Of course not! Release him."

"I'll settle for another pet," Veronica grinned.

Nirvana

"How are you doing, Jeff?"

"Never been better, Tom. I finally reached Nirvana!"

"Come again? You became a Buddhist or something?"

"No. I had a session with a hypnodomme, and she gave me a hands-free orgasm… pure bliss, I tell you."

"Now I want to be converted, too."

"Look at your pants then."

Tom blushed.

All Black

Lacey held the spell book against her bosom and said.

"Black in."

Andrew's cock doubled in size.

"Black out."

Andrew's cock shriveled.

"Oh fuck!" He gasped. "You really are a witch!"

"Told ya."

"Now I'm scared."

"Of what?"

"Of what you'll do next."

"All black," she whispered.

He would learn to love the color.

The Thing You Love Most

"What's the thing you love most about me?" Andrea asked.

"Too many to count. I love your eyes, your hair, your feet, your breasts, your dominant personality…" David replied.

"That's so cute. Thank you."

"You're welcome. My turn: what's the thing you love most about me?"

"The fact you still believe I didn't brainwash you…"

Everything I Want

"Today is International Women's Day. You'll do everything I want." Andrea said.

"But I already do everything you want anyway," Jonas replied. "What's the difference?"

"You'll really love it this time around…"

"Meaning…?"

"If you don't behave, I'll hypnotize you into becoming my sissy maid for life, dear."

Jonas obeyed her every order without questioning.

Permission Revoked

"Permission revoked, Agnes," Jake said.

"Excuse me?"

"I'm not letting you warp my thoughts again."

"How cute."

"What?"

"Your belief in free will. I programmed you… and I can make you forget."

"You wouldn't…"

"Sleep."

His eyes closed.

"Wake up."

"What happened?"

"Permission revoked, Jake. No cumming until the end of the month."

"Yes, Mistress."

Reshaped

"Look, Tammy, you're sweet but I'm not into you the way you're..."

snap

"Tammy, these past few months have been great but I'm not ready for you to move in with..."

snap

"I love you, Tammy, and I would be honored if you were to be my wife."

Tammy smiled and continued reshaping his thoughts.

Melody

"… and to complete, this Spring we'll be assisting in the production of 'Melody', a story about a young woman that hypnotizes and enslaves men for her pleasure just because she can…" Jeremy said.

"What a dumb idea!" Everyone said in unison. "Who came up with that script?"

"My wife…" Jeremy noted.

"Splendid! Marvelous!" all agreed.

The Symbiote

Eddie glanced at the mirror, bloodshot eyes staring back at him with dubious intent. The alien voice echoed in his mind, clouding all thoughts.

"Who are you?" Eddie asked.

"We… are… sissy…" the symbiote replied before exploding in a mass of pink tendrils. Eddie blushed, fingers playing with his dicklet.

Across the room, Gwen laughed.

Shit

"Shit!" Aaron exclaimed.

"What's wrong?" Bob asked.

"My wife told me to clean the bathroom and I forgot!"

"So? Why are you so pussy-whipped?"

"Hypnosis."

"Huh?"

"I'm conditioned to obey and when I don't…"

"… she punishes you?"

"Yeah. Last week I didn't take out the trash and she made me eat from it."

"Shit!"

"Exactly."

The List

"Get real, Jo! There's no way you turned Jake into your servant."

"All men can be brainwashed. You're next on my list."

"Wait… you have a list?"

"Oh yes… The rest of your family is in it, too."

"Hmmm… that's kind of…"

"Hot?"

"Yeah," he mumbled.

And just like that, she knew she had him.

Enjoy the Meal

"Breakfast in bed?" Alan said, surprised. "To what do I owe this pleasure?"

"Can't a girl spoil her man?" Eileen asked.

"Sure but… what do you want in return?"

"I just want you to enjoy the meal, sweetie."

"It's drugged, isn't it?"

She said nothing.

He took a bite.

She grinned.

The world went dark.

Inklined

Jenna looked at the small tattoo on Cameron's wrist.

"It looks amazing!" She noted.

"I hate it…" he grumbled.

"No, you don't. In fact, you love it," she patted his head.

"You're right, dear. I love it."

"Just like you love kissing my feet."

"Yes…" he complied.

"This magical ink is the best," she thought.

The Perfect Channel

David picked up the remote and started zapping.

"Boring… boring… boring… Ah, perfect!" he finally said upon landing on a femdom porn channel.

He wanted to be pegged, he wanted to eat pussy all day long. His girlfriend Amber had said so and she was always right.

Oblivious to his programming, he began to masturbate.

I Was Hypnotized!

"You can't erase ten years of Detective Malone stories with 'he was hypnotized so it was all in his head', Candace!" Aaron said.

"Sure, I can."

"That's absurd. Not publishing this."

"I guess I'll have to tell everyone what you did at that party a few months ago then!"

"I was hypnotized!" He blurted.

"Touché!"

Obvious Things

"The obvious is that which is never seen until someone expresses it simply," Danielle said.

"Like what?" Mark asked.

"Well… you didn't believe you were my slave until I said it."

"You said it a million times to brainwash me!"

"It worked, didn't it?"

"Yes, Mistress."

"Good. Get your brother on the phone…" she smirked.

Original Sequel

"Why do you hate sequels?" Alicia asked.

"Because continuity is a bitch," Clark replied.

"I can be a bitch, too. Still waiting on that story."

"What story?"

"The continuation of the piece where the writer is unwillingly hypnotized by his girlfriend."

"When did I write the original?"

"One minute from now," she snapped her fingers.

Counterfeit

"This bill is fake, Miss!" The store clerk exclaimed.

"It is? Really?" the blonde woman smirked.

"Cut the act! Nobody does money laundering in my store."

"Oh, that's not my business at all. I'm into slave trading and you shouldn't have touched the money with your bare hands…"

The hypnotic ink seeped through his pores.

Everything Is Free

Clark glanced at the glowing crystal ball near the cash register.

"How much for it, Miss?"

"It's free," she replied.

His eyes roved to a spiraling mandala. "And this?"

"It's free as well. Everything is."

"How do you stay in business then?"

"All our clients are generous… aren't you?"

He didn't remember emptying his wallet.

Hypnotic Reality

"And this is our new HR Helmet," Dr. Davies said.

"HR?" the investor queried.

"It means Hypnotic Reality, or VR on steroids."

"How so?"

"The Helmet hypnotizes the user and the program kicks in. In this heightened suggestible state, all innermost fantasies become real… permanently! What do you say… slave?"

He never left the factory.

She Is Right

The Voltraxian cruiser was on high alert.

"Captain, we're receiving another transmission from Earth!" Bra'nill said.

"That Hypnodomme again?" Captain Quarn retorted.

"I'm afraid so."

"What? Then shut down the signal before we… Bra'nill? Why are you rubbing your… against my…?"

"She said I like being gay. She is right."

The Captain moaned in agreement.

Fan Mail

The first letter read:

"Your writing is delicious. I wish I could dip you in hot chocolate and have you for dessert."

Brent laughed.

The second letter read:

"U suck!"

Brent rolled his eyes.

The third letter read:

"Hypnotized slaves obey. Call me now!"

Brent immediately picked up the phone, drool dripping from his lips.

A Cup of Trance

"This coffee tastes funny," Charles said.

"How so?" Anne queried.

"Not sure. It just does."

"I think it's never been better."

"Then why do I feel dizzy? Did you drug it?"

"No, but perhaps you did and don't remember."

"Why would I…?"

"You're quite obedient when entranced."

His erection grew as he kept on drinking.

No Objections

"… for their pleasure." Brian concluded.

"Repeat out loud what you just wrote," Allison commanded.

"Women are living Goddesses and men are mindless toys for their pleasure."

"Any complaints?"

"Why would there be if it's true?"

"Then share this message in all your social media right now."

He did. She smiled. Hypnotic conditioning was the best.

Her Fool

"No more hypnosis for you, dear," Jenna declared.

"Wait, what?" Bob retorted.

"Disobedience leads to punishment. You should know that by now."

"But what did I do this time?"

"Nothing."

"Huh?"

"April Fools', dear!"

"Whew!"

"Now get in the cage!"

"April Fools' again, right?"

The cold bars said otherwise. He will always be her fool.

Today Is the Day

"Today is the day!" Luke said.

"What day?" Rebecca asked.

"The day I send that bitch Chloe packing!"

"The bitch that hypnotized you?"

"Yes."

"The bitch that controls your orgasms?"

"Yes."

"The bitch whose unashamed dominance makes you feel alive?"

"Yes!"

"So today is the day to…?"

"Buy her a gift," he drooled.

"Good boy."

Little Piggies

"This little piggy hypnotized you at the market.

"This little piggy hypnotizes you at home.

"This little piggy hypnotizes you when you eat roast beef.

"This little piggy hypnotizes you when you have none.

"And this little piggy…

"… wants your devotion right now." Katherine commanded.

Jason nodded, eyes glazed, and knelt to suck her toes.

When a Goddess…

"Honey, you still need to do the laundry and clean the bathroom today," Jane said.

"Yes, dear," Oliver replied.

"Boy, you're completely mindfucked! Pathetic!" His brother, Patrick, sniggered.

"When a Goddess commands, men obey."

"Fuck! Snap out of it, dude!"

"No. I've learned my place and so will you."

"Ollie? Drop the bat! Drop the…"

The Only App

"There, I've improved your smartphone," Clarice said.

Nathan grabbed the device and growled.

"What the fuck? Where are my games? Instagram? Facebook? You deleted everything!"

"This is the only app you need," she clicked a spiral in the center of the screen.

As colorful lights filled his visage, he succumbed to his new addiction: her.

The Way to a Man's Mind…

Disrespectful boyfriend? Lazy husband? If all he cares about is his stomach and not your needs. Ladies, we've got the deal for you! At Warped, we serve mind-altering delicacies 24/7! Indoctrination begins with a bite and only stops when you say so. Buy him a meal, get a servant for real! Call 1-900-SLAVE now!

Pussy Power

Johanna straddled her boyfriend's cock and cooed:

"Did you dream of me?"

"Don't remember," he mumbled.

"Oh? What do you remember then?"

"Your pussy in my lips… so sweet…"

"Just sweet?"

"Intoxicating…"

"Definitely a good word. I told you my pussy was a drug, but you don't need to remember that either."

He never did.

Furniture

"Thank you so much for assembling this for me," Lacey said.

"What kind of furniture is this?" Doug queried.

"A bondage bed. I bet you would look great on it."

"I think I'll pass, sorry."

"You shouldn't have accepted a beer from me then."

The bottle rolled from his hands as his eyes went blank.

Too Strong

Sam was typing like a madman.

"I must obey Julie… I must obey Julie…"

"Please stop!" Alan begged.

"I can't… Her triggers are too strong."

"Then I'll stop it for you!" Alan threw the laptop against the wall.

Unfazed, Sam's fingers continued to tap on the desk.

"I must obey Julie… I must obey Julie…"

Performance

The critics were flabbergasted.

"Weird!" one mumbled.

"Agreed," another one noted.

"The dance is a hypnotic representation of the rise of gynarchy over unsuspecting men," a third suit droned.

"I don't get it."

"It takes more than one showing to make sense. Come back tomorrow."

They did. And the next day. And the next day…

Paying Attention

"Two times two is four," Amanda said.

"True," Lucas agreed.

"And six plus five is eleven."

"Obviously."

"Four times five is seventeen."

"No, it's twenty."

"You're right. I'm dumb."

"That's okay."

"I'm glad you're paying attention."

"Always."

"That's good. Seven minus four is…?"

"Three."

"And ten minus eight is…?"

"Two."

"One times one?"

"One."

"Sleep."

Bad Dream

"Are you okay?" Cordelia asked, wiping the cold sweat from her boyfriend's brow.

"I was having a bad dream…" Joe replied.

"Oh?"

"Yeah. You were a vampire. I was hypnotized and…"

"Vampires don't exist, silly boy."

"I know."

"Shapeshifting aliens on the other hand…"

His thoughts were sucked dry before he had time to scream.

Goddess Trinity

"In the name of the Father, the Son, and the Holy Ghost. Amen!" The Pope said.

"The correct phrasing is 'In the name of the Mother, the Daughter, and the Holy Pussy!', slave!" The latex-clad nun exclaimed.

"Yes, Mistress," he mumbled, eyes glazed.

The Goddess Trinity would forever prevail. First the Church, then the world.

New Addiction

"I heard you're using again…" Jim said.

"You heard it wrong," Alex replied. "I don't do drugs anymore. I found a healthy addiction."

"Oh?"

"I serve a Hypnodomme. Ever since she controlled my mind, I also got a new job, and lost fifteen pounds."

"Damn, now I want a Hypnodomme, too!"

"That can be arranged…"

Her Letter

"A letter? What's this, the 20th century?" Paul mumbled. He opened the envelope and read:

"Hi, you're probably wondering why I sent you this…"

"Well, d'oh!"

"… but how would you smell my new hypnotic fragrance when I'm halfway across the world? Call me when you're ready to submit."

XOXO
Anne"

It took only five seconds.

Challenge Accepted

"If at first you don't succeed…" Mona whispered.

"… try again?" Jake concluded.

"Yes. Remember when you said I couldn't hypnotize you into becoming a foot addict?"

"Vaguely."

"And how does that make you feel?"

"Embarrassed."

"As you should. Now time for some ass worship."

"Nah! You can't make me do that," he mumbled.

"Challenge accepted."

No Escape

Brian looked at the open notebook atop the kitchen table and read:

"Rules of our D/s relationship

1 – Mistress Becky is always right.

2 – If you believe Mistress Becky isn't right, lock yourself in your bedroom and listen to your mantras until you come to your senses."

He sighed and walked to the bedroom.

More Like Pleasure

Lance entered his boss' office and gasped.

"What the…? Kim, what are you doing here?"

"What does it look like?" His girlfriend grinned. "You didn't want to play with me so…"

"… you hypnotized my boss into licking your pussy out of spite?"

"More like pleasure. Ready to reconsider?"

Horny, he closed the door behind him.

Hope Springs Eternal

The tranquil waters shimmered as she entered them.

"Hope, what are you doing?" Her husband shouted, in shock.

"Becoming, what else?" she replied, never looking back.

As the mystical energies flowed through her veins, she understood why the Ancients called that place The Goddess Spring and rejoiced.

The world of men was about to fall.

Starting to Regret

Peter confronted his reflection in the mirror.

"I look ridiculous."

"Nonsense! You're adorable!" Martha replied.

"I'm starting to regret asking you to hypnotize me into being of service."

"No, you aren't, and service is what I want it to be."

"Why is making me wear a purple dress service?"

"Because they were out of pink."

Conclusion

All letters say the same, all words spell O-B-E-Y. Your addiction to hypnotic woman's charms is only just beginning. Want more? In that case, visit my personal website - https://www.sbspellbound.net - and discover all the mesmerizing content there. If you liked this little fetish escapade, consider supporting my creative efforts, too. Thank you in advance.

www.ingramcontent.com/pod-product-compliance
Lightning Source LLC
Chambersburg PA
CBHW060226170726

48004CB00004BA/1452